Dear Parent:
Your child's love of reading starts here!

Every child learns to read in a different way and at his or her own speed. You can help your young reader improve and become more confident by encouraging his or her own interests and abilities. You can also guide your child's spiritual development by reading stories with biblical values and Bible stories, like I Can Read! books published by Zonderkidz. From books your child reads with you to the first books he or she reads alone, there are I Can Read! books for every stage of reading:

SHARED READING
Basic language, word repetition, and whimsical illustrations, ideal for sharing with your emergent reader.

BEGINNING READING
Short sentences, familiar words, and simple concepts for children eager to read on their own.

READING WITH HELP
Engaging stories, longer sentences, and language play for developing readers.

READING ALONE
Complex plots, challenging vocabulary, and high-interest topics for the independent reader.

ADVANCED READING
Short paragraphs, chapters, and exciting themes for the perfect bridge to chapter books.

I Can Read! books have introduced children to the joy of reading since 1957. Featuring award-winning authors and illustrators and a fabulous cast of beloved characters, I Can Read! books set the standard for beginning readers.

A lifetime of discovery begins with the magical words **"I Can Read!"**

Visit www.icanread.com for information on enriching your child's reading experience.
Visit www.zonderkidz.com for more Zonderkidz I Can Read! titles.

... For the LORD will be at your side
and will keep your foot from being snared.
—Proverbs 3:26

ZONDERKIDZ

Junior Battles to Be His Best
Copyright © 2011 Big Idea Entertainment, LLC. VEGGIETALES®, character
names, likenesses and other indicia are trademarks of and copyrighted by Big Idea
Entertainment, LLC. All rights reserved.
Illustrations © 2011 by Big Idea Entertainment, Inc.

Requests for information should be addressed to:
Zonderkidz, *Grand Rapids, Michigan 49530*

ISBN 978-0-310-72732-3

Editor: Mary Hassinger
Art direction: Karen Poth
Cover design: Karen Poth
Interior design: Ron Eddy

Printed in China

ZONDERkidz

I Can Read!

BEGINNING
1
READING

Junior Battles to Be His Best

story by Karen Poth

Junior's dad was reading the newspaper.
"Junior," he said, "here's a story about
the Bumblyburg Battle of the Bands!"

"You and your friends should enter,"
Dad said.

"No, Dad," Junior said. "I don't want to play
my tuba. Everyone will laugh at me."

Junior's mom convinced him to try.

"You just have to practice," Mom said.

"You'll see. A little hard work
will pay off!"

Junior tried. But he got frustrated.

"It's too hard," Junior said.

"I'm not going to do it."

The next day,

Jimmy and Jerry saw the

Battle of the Bands poster.

They found Junior at The Hop.

Jimmy and Jerry asked Junior to help

get a band together.

"No," Junior said.

"I'm not going to do it.

It's just too hard."

Jimmy and Jerry were sad.
But they decided to do it
even if Junior wouldn't help.

All the next week,
Junior saw his friends practicing
with their bands.

On Monday, he saw Jenny Gourd's band,

The Bubblegum Pop Rockers.

They practiced at the playground.

On Tuesday, Junior saw

Larry and the Peas.

Their band was called Heavy Metal.

Larry was the drummer.

He looked so cool!

On Wednesday, Junior heard

Pa Grape's band, The Space Cadets.

They sounded pretty good.

But they looked a little funny.

Junior started to feel left out.

Then Junior saw Ma Mushroom.

"Are you playing in the battle?" Ma asked.

"No," Junior said. "I'm not good enough."

Ma Mushroom smiled.

"Good," she said. "Then we'll win for sure! It sounds like you already beat yourself!"

"What do you mean?" Junior asked.

"Well, if you don't try,

then you've already lost," Ma said.

Junior felt terrible.

Ma Mushroom was right.

He had not even tried.

When Junior got home

he practiced his tuba.

And he practiced some more …

"Junior," his mom said, "you are really sounding great! Maybe next year you'll enter the battle of the bands!"

"No, Mom," Junior said.

"I don't think I'm good enough."

"Why don't you pray about it?" Mom said.

That night, Junior asked God
to give him courage to play
in front of others some day!

Finally, it was Saturday,

the day of the big battle.

The whole town was there.

Everyone played very well.

In the end only two bands were left—

Jimmy and Jerry's Blues Band

and Ma Mushroom's Swingers!

"We have a tie!" the judge said.

"You will each play one more song.

  Give it ALL you've got!"

Jimmy ran out in the audience.

He found Junior.

"Junior, we need you," Jimmy said.

Junior jumped up with a smile.

He went to the stage.

He played his best.

It was just what the Blues Band needed.

Jimmy and Jerry's Blues Band won!

And so did Junior!

"Thank you for your help, God!"

Junior prayed.